CALAMITY KATE

TERRY DEARY

ILLUSTRATED BY
CHARLOTTE FIRMIN

A & C BL

Black Cats

The Ramsbottom Rumble • Georgia Byng
Calamity Kate • Terry Deary
Ghost Town • Terry Deary
The Custard Kid • Terry Deary
The Treasure of Crazy Horse • Terry Deary
Dear Ms • Joan Poulson
It's a Tough Life • Jeremy Strong
Big Iggy • Kaye Umansky

First paperback edition 2001
First published in hardback 1980 by
A & C Black (Publishers) Ltd
37 Soho Square, London W1D 3QZ

ISBN 0-7136-5988-2

A CIP catalogue for this book is available from the British Library.

Printed and bound in Spain by G. Z. Printek, Bilbao.

I

'Oooh! Aaagh! Oooh!'

It was dark. It was quiet, apart from the muffled cries of the helpless young lady. 'Oooh! Aaagh! Oooh!' she cried, and well she might; for her feet were tightly bound with rope and her hands were firmly lashed to a railway line. 'Oooh! Aaagh! Oooh!' she groaned as she struggled to free herself. There was fear in her eyes; there was a sock in her mouth.

Then through the dim evening air came the sad wail of a distant train; the young lady struggled desperately to free at least one hand, but the strength was draining from her aching body and her cries grew weaker as terror (and the large woollen sock) dried her mouth.

Suddenly through the gloom there loomed the locomotive, rushing towards her at fearful speed. All seemed lost as the young lady swooned away in a dead faint. But through the darkness came the powerful cry of a man's voice which drowned even the dreadful thunder of the dashing train:

'O.K. Cut!'

The image of the train vanished from the screen; the young lady sighed and smiled a woollen smile; the lights came up brightly in the film studio.

Willing helpers hurried to untie the young actress from the painted wooden railway line, while the film director, the famous Mr Otto Premiere, strolled over to compliment her on her beautiful performance.

'Well, Mr Premiere?' she asked hopefully. 'How was I?'

'Miss Kate,' he answered seriously, looking over the top of his wire-rimmed spectacles. 'You were perfect.'

'Oh, Mr Premiere, you're too kind,' she murmured, as she blushed prettily till the red of her cheeks almost matched the burning red of her hair.

He shook his head firmly. 'No, I'm not kind,' he snapped.

'Oh, no, Mr Premiere,' agreed the confused Kate.

'Can't afford to be kind in the film business,' he went on sternly.

'Of course not, Mr Premiere.'

'I can make you the biggest star in Hollywood,' he grunted.

'Cooo!' gasped Kate, her blue eyes swimming dreamily at the thought.

'But I'll make *myself* a lot of money at the same time,' he rasped.

He turned and began to stalk away as Kate swallowed hard, and found the nerve to ask him, 'Excuse me, Mr Premiere, but when do I start?'

Otto Premiere stopped, turned and growled, 'Tomorrow morning, at seven o'clock. The film's called *The Dangers of Daphne*, and you play the part of Daphne.' He almost allowed a smile to warm up his grey face as he added, 'Yes, I'm going to make you a star.'

'A star,' crooned Kate, and with a sigh of happiness she fainted.

2

Hunk Marvel

Miss Kate, or Calamity Kate as she was known to her friends, had been in the famous film-making town of Hollywood for just over three weeks. Every day she had walked wearily around the film studios searching for work, or even an audition so that she could show her talents as an actress.

But at every studio the answer had been the same: 'No work today.' She had left her home town of Deadwood with such high hopes of being a star; but three weeks of failure had left her with empty dreams and an even emptier purse. All she had to look forward to was the heartache of having to sell her jewels to buy a ticket back to Deadwood.

Tired and hungry she had left her hotel that morning and decided that she would have one last try to find work; if it failed then she would give up and go home.

And so it was that she had arrived at the huge wooden barn that served as the studio of a film company known as 'Warmer Sisters', to hear the magical words: 'Yes, you can have an audition.'

The exhausting struggle of playing a girl tied to a railway track and the shock of being given the part had been too much for her; she had fainted.

She slowly came round to find a strong arm about her shoulders lifting her from the floor so that she could sip the glass of brandy at her lips. She half opened her eyes, afraid that she was waking from a dream, to discover that the strong arm belonged to a slim young man dressed as a cowboy.

'Custard,' murmured Kate in a daze.

'Custard?' came the smooth strange voice of the young man. 'Well, no, it's brandy actually.'

Kate's eyes flew wide open when she realised that the young man was a stranger. 'Oh . . . er . . . sorry,' she gasped, 'I mean I thought that *you* were Custard.'

The young man raised his eyebrows and smiled, revealing a set of teeth as perfect as the keyboard of a new piano. 'But my dear, how on earth could you mistake me for a bowl of custard?' He looked up, smiling at the group of studio-hands who had gathered round; everyone laughed heartily at his remark as though he had said the funniest thing imaginable.

Kate became even more confused and struggled to her feet feeling very foolish. 'What I meant to say,' she went on hurriedly, 'was that I have a friend called the Custard Kid, and you look rather like him.'

'Good Lord!' exclaimed the young man in a lazy, musical voice. 'Heaven forbid that I should look like someone called *Custard*!' Again he smiled at the circle of people around him, and again they laughed in chorus.

'Oh, but he's awfully nice, really,' said Kate, a little annoyed that these strangers were making fun of the name of her dearest friend.

The young man sensed her annoyance and turned his charming smile upon Kate. 'Of course he is, my dear,' he cooed. 'But let's not argue over a little thing like that. You and I must become friends.' He took Kate's hand and gazed deeply into her eyes. Kate felt her heart flutter with mixed feelings of admiration and fear for this overpowering man, as he said gently, 'Yes, really good friends, my dear, if we are to work together.'

'But who are you?' asked the surprised Kate.

The young man took a step backwards and looked a little shocked and very hurt. 'You mean you don't recognise me?' he asked in return. 'My name is . . . ' and here he paused to let the full importance of the name sink into Kate's mind. 'My name is Hunk Marvel!'

Kate's mouth fell open in surprise and wonder. Hunk was obviously very pleased at the effect his name had upon Kate, and went on to explain that he was to be the star of the film *The Dangers of Daphne*. Kate was a little puzzled by this and asked, 'Does that mean that you are playing the part of Daphne? But I thought that I was. . . .'

Hunk Marvel snapped back at her a little crossly, 'Don't be stupid!' He quickly calmed his flutter of annoyance and with the skill of a star actor he turned on his charming act for Kate once more. He explained patiently as if he were talking to a three-year-old. 'You don't understand my dear,' he began. 'The film is a serial called *The Dangers of Daphne*; but Daphne is a rather foolish child who, at the end of each episode, finds herself in extreme peril. It is then up to *me*, the poor but honest hero, to rescue the silly girl each time.'

'Oh, I see,' said Kate. 'I'm sorry if I was a little slow to understand, but Mr Premiere didn't explain. . . .'

'No, he wouldn't, the miserable old trout,' replied Hunk spitefully. 'Don't let old Premiere worry you. Why, *I* could produce better films than *him*.'

'But I thought that he was the best producer in Hollywood,' muttered the confused Kate.

'Only because he's lucky enough to have the best *actors* in his films,' replied Hunk firmly.

'You mean. . . .'

'Yes,' cut in the young actor. He lifted his chin a little and looked proudly down his long nose at Calamity Kate. 'He has such wonderful actors as *me*.'

'Coo!' gasped Kate. Hunk was obviously pleased to have won her admiration, and said, 'Don't worry, my dear. Stick with me. I'm going to make you a star.'

Kate's heart gave a jump as she heard these words for the second time that day.

But this time she did not faint.

3

The Warmer Sisters

'Excuse me, but is your name Miss Calamity Kate?' asked a studio messenger boy.

'Why, yes,' answered Kate, coming out of her daydream.

'I have a message for you from the Sisters. They want you to sign a contract as soon as possible,' explained the boy.

'The Sisters?' asked Kate, 'Who are the Sisters?'

'Oh, he means the Warmer Sisters, my dear,' put in Hunk Marvel. 'They own the studios, you know. Their office is just over the road. Come along, I'll show you.'

Kate allowed herself to be led to the small, but richly furnished offices of the Warmer Sisters; she knocked timidly at the door of the Sisters' private office, and after a moment a strong voice boomed, 'Come in!' She nervously opened the door, and came face to face with the famous Warmer Sisters.

'Do come in and take a seat,' said a delicate, grey-haired woman who smiled gently at Kate. 'My name is Minnie Warmer, and I'm in charge of the film-making.' Kate smiled back and at once felt at ease in the company of the quiet, kindly Minnie.

'Pleased to meet you Miss Minnie, I'm sure,' replied Kate, as she sank into a deep, velvet-covered armchair.

'My name's Gertrude Warmer,' boomed the frighteningly loud voice of the other Warmer sister. Kate looked up to meet the fierce stare of the second and much more remarkable sister, Gertrude. The young actress struggled to her feet to shake the outstretched hand of Gertrude Warmer and winced with pain as she felt her hand clasped in a grip of iron.

With a little sigh of relief Kate recovered her hand and returned shakily to her seat. Just as Minnie Warmer was gentle and ladylike so Gertrude Warmer was tough and manly; Minnie's hair fell in natural grey waves, while

Gertrude's was cropped short with a dead-straight fringe and dyed a harsh, unreal black. The black of her hair made her face, caked thickly with make-up powder, look like a mask, and the gash of brilliant red lipstick looked like a rather nasty accident.

'I'm in charge of the business side of Warmer Sisters,' said the beefy Gertrude in her voice like a big bass bell. 'Just sign these papers will you?'

'Oh, but shouldn't I read them first?' asked Kate, shakily.

'Humph! Can if you want to,' snorted Gertrude.

'Of course you must dear,' agreed Minnie softly. 'You may find all the legal language a little hard to follow, so I'll explain it to you.'

'No need, Minnie,' grunted Gertrude. 'Contracts are my business. I'll explain.' Gertrude leaned over Kate to explain the documents and Kate discovered that not only was Miss Warmer's appearance overpowering; the strong smell of too much cheap perfume was rather overpowering too.

'First part says that you agree to work for no one else but Warmer Sisters for at least one year,' Gertrude Warmer snapped briskly. 'Sign here.' Kate did so meekly.

'Second part says that we agree to pay you one hundred dollars.'

Kate's mouth fell open in wonder at the thought. 'One *hundred* dollars!' she murmured dreamily. 'One hundred dollars a year.' It was more money than she had ever seen before.

Gertrude sighed heavily. 'No, no, no. That's one hundred dollars a *week*.'

Kate signed hastily before she woke up to find it was all a dream.

'Lastly your insurance.'

'Insurance? Why do I need insurance?' asked Kate uncertainly.

'You don't,' replied Gertrude impatiently, 'but we do.'

'I don't understand,' said the confused Kate.

'It's like this,' began Gertrude. 'Just suppose we were six weeks on this film and spent a fortune on hiring actors like Hunk Marvel, not to mention the cameramen and the film and the rent for the studio. And then suppose that *you* had an accident and the film was never finished. What would *we* get back from the film for all our expense?' asked Gertrude like a school mistress talking to a stupid pupil.

'Er, nothing?' suggested Kate.

'Precisely,' answered Gertrude. 'And so we need insurance. If you have an accident and can't finish the film then the insurance company will pay for our losses.'

'How marvellous!' exclaimed Kate. 'And how

much am I insured for?' she ventured to ask.

'That's none of your business,' growled Gertrude angrily.

'Oh, I don't see why she shouldn't know,' cut in Minnie quietly but firmly. 'We want you to take very great care of yourself my dear. You see, you are insured for a million dollars.'

Kate was still dazed by the idea of being worth a million dollars to someone, as Minnie showed her to the door and told her to get a good night's sleep so that she would be fresh and ready for work at seven o'clock the next morning. 'You know Mr Premiere is a hard man to work for but he is a brilliant producer,' she explained with a smile.

'Oh, but Hunk Marvel said that he...' began Kate.

Minnie placed a finger to her lips to silence Kate and looked nervously over her shoulder towards Gertrude who was studying papers at the desk. 'Yes, dear,' whispered Minnie hurriedly, 'Mr Premiere and Hunk Marvel don't get on at all well.'

'Then why does he use him in his films?' asked Kate a little too loudly, so that Gertrude looked up sharply from her desk.

Minnie opened the door to hurry Kate out. Just as she closed it Minnie said quietly, 'Hunk Marvel is only a star because my sister Gertrude wants him to be.' The door closed and Kate turned away puzzling over this new piece of information. It was then that she noticed the tall thin cowboy sitting on the chair outside the door.

'Oh,' Kate exclaimed. 'You waited for me Hunk. That was kind of you.'

The cowboy stood up and turned to face Kate. Kate blinked in disbelief for several seconds then she threw her arms around his neck and hugged him till his hat fell off.

'Custard!' she yelled. 'It *is* you Custard!'

4

The Custard Kid

The Custard Kid recovered his breath, and his hat, and grinned at Calamity Kate. 'Well, Miss Kate, what are *you* doing here?'

'I was just going to ask you the same thing!' exclaimed Kate. 'I'm here because I'm going to be a star in *The Dangers of Daphne* and they're paying me a hundred dollars a week and I thought that Hunk Marvel was you and then I thought you were Hunk Marvel,' she gabbled.

'Well here I am, just bursting to hear you, but slow it down,' he pleaded. Kate took a deep breath and told her story to her best friend the Custard Kid. Custard listened with growing excitement, then said to Kate, 'You know, it's funny you should think I look like Hunk Marvel, because that's just what that director fellow said.'

'You mean Mr Premiere?' asked Kate.

'That's right. Mr Premiere. He said he was looking for someone like me to act as a stunt-man to do all the dangerous stunts in Hunk Marvel's next film.'

'Oooh,' gasped Kate, 'won't that be dangerous?'

'Oh, not really,' said Custard modestly. 'Just a bit of falling off horses, fighting grizzly bears single-handed, rescuing a trainload of people from quicksand and little things like that.'

'Why can't Hunk Marvel do those things himself?' asked Kate, who was a little worried at the risks her friend was going to have to run.

'Well,' replied Custard, 'it seems that Mr Hunk Marvel isn't as brave as he appears in the films. He always has to have a stunt-man to do the dangerous tricks for him. But Mr Premiere was extra pleased because I look so much like Hunk Marvel that no one will be able to tell the difference.'

'That's true,' agreed Kate. Suddenly she jumped up to hug the Custard Kid once more. 'Oooh,' she cried, 'it's great to think that we'll be working together on the same film. You go in and see the Warmer Sisters about your contract and I'll see you tomorrow morning in the studio.'

As Calamity Kate lay in bed that night excited thoughts chased each other through her mind. A movie star ... handsome Hunk Marvel ... a hundred dollars ... *The Dangers of Daphne* ... and dear old Custard....

She fell asleep with a smile on her face.

5

Daphne in Danger

Kate arrived at the studio at five minutes to seven the following morning to find that Mr Premiere and his film crew had already been there for an hour setting up the scene.

'Nice to see that *some* of my actors can arrive on time,' grunted Mr Premiere. He led Kate over to a tall thin stranger dressed entirely in black and introduced him. 'This is one of your co-stars, Mr Abel Sourgrape. Abel plays the part of the villain in this movie.'

Kate shook hands a little nervously with the sour-faced Abel Sourgrape, while Abel looked sharply at Kate with his narrow green eyes under heavy black eyebrows. Mr Premiere remarked bitterly, 'Of course your other co-star, Mr Hunk Marvel, hasn't honoured us with his

presence yet.' A little spitefully he added, 'I believe that he finds great difficulty in dragging himself from his warm bed on these chilly autumn mornings.'

'You don't like Hunk, do you Mr Premiere?' asked Kate.

'I like any actor or actress who works hard and gives his or her best at all times,' he answered, bitterly.

Kate changed the subject and asked brightly, 'Which scene are we filming today Mr Premiere?'

In reply Otto Premiere led her over to a huge water tank, about a metre deep and so large that it took up the whole of one end of the studio.

'Today's scene,' began the director, 'begins when the villain of the story, played by Abel Sourgrape here, pushes poor Daphne, played by you, into a fast-flowing crocodile-infested river.'

Kate looked doubtfully at the calm tank, but Mr Premiere went on to explain that a large paddle machine would be switched on to make the water look rough and fierce. Kate's job was to thrash about in the water, screaming, as a crocodile slid into the water and swam towards her.

'Ooh, but won't that be dangerous?' gasped Kate.

Mr Premiere allowed a rare smile to brighten his face, and explained that it would in fact be a wooden model of a crocodile in the tank with her. Kate sighed with relief, and became excited by the task ahead of her.

'And how do I ... er, I mean how does Daphne escape from the crocodile?' she asked.

'How do you think?' asked Abel Sourgrape in a silky smooth voice, raising one bushy eyebrow questioningly.

Calamity Kate screwed up her face and thought hard. At last she said in a fierce, determined voice, 'Well, if I were Daphne I'd punch the old croc on the snout and send him off with his tail between his legs.'

'Ah, but you're not Daphne,' hissed Abel in his best villain voice which sent a small shiver down Kate's back. 'Daphne is weak and helpless....'

'What!' exclaimed Kate. 'Can't she stick up for herself?'

Abel Sourgrape shook his head.

'Humph!' snorted Kate in disgust. 'In that case she deserves to be eaten.'

'Ah, but the audiences wouldn't like to see a pretty young lady torn to shreds,' teased the villain.

'Then what *do* they want?' grumbled Kate.

'They want to see her rescued by the tall dark

and handsome hero,' put in Otto Premiere. 'Unfortunately *our* hero is Mr Marvel and even if he were here he wouldn't be much use.'

'Why not?'

'He can't even swim,' replied Mr Premiere in disgust. He sighed then said, 'However we do have the services of an excellent stunt-man. He looks just like Hunk Marvel too. He'll dive in, stab your wooden crocodile with a wooden knife, then drag you to the river bank. Come along and meet him; his name is. . . .'

'The Custard Kid,' put in Kate brightly.

'You know him?' asked the director in surprise.

'Oh, sure,' answered Kate happily. 'We're old friends.'

Calamity Kate and the Custard Kid greeted each other cheerfully and chatted while the final touches were put to the scene. The bright studio lights glared over the tank and the paddle machine rumbled into life to make the surface of the water appear rough and dangerous. At the far side of the tank cardboard rocks and trees had been carefully arranged to look like a river bank and it was here that Kate and Abel Sourgrape placed themselves in readiness to begin the scene.

Otto Premiere called 'Action!' And the cameras began to roll.

6

Kate in Danger

'Unhand me villain!' cried Calamity Kate as Abel Sourgrape struggled to cast her into the foaming water. Actually it wouldn't have mattered if Kate had cried, 'What a lovely day for a swim,' because it was a silent movie and her words were not recorded. But Kate used the sort of words she imagined Daphne might have said and it helped her to act in a realistic way: too realistic. More than once Kate's struggles almost forced the sweating Abel Sourgrape into the tank, until at last he was forced to use a rather nasty trick. He placed his foot behind Kate and pushed very hard.

With a gasp of surprise Kate tumbled backwards into the frothy water and hit it with a splash that soaked the villain from head to toe. Kate's mouth was still open in a roar of anger as her head went under the water. She stood up spitting out water (and some very unladylike words) at the sopping Sourgrape.

Just in time Kate remembered that she was supposed to be the helpless Daphne and began struggling and screaming like a drowning girl. Abel Sourgrape disappeared from the scene to be replaced by a new threat. A trapdoor was opened behind the cardboard rocks and the snout of a crocodile appeared.

'Oh, my,' thought Kate as she looked up to see the crocodile approach, 'doesn't that dummy crocodile look real!' She began to thrash and scream as hard as she could, 'Oh help, it's a *crocodile*!' As Kate screamed the crocodile seemed to move its head ever so slightly and fix two beady, greedy eyes upon her. A pink tongue slid over a set of razor-sharp teeth to lick the pale green lips.

And Kate's cries changed.

'Oh, no. It *is* a crocodile. It really *is* a crocodile!'

Kate turned and tried to make for the side of the tank. The water was only just over a metre deep but Kate's long heavy dress was soaked and dragged at her legs. Like those nightmares

where you turn to run from the monster, only to find yourself running through treacle, she pushed and struggled but moved barely at all.

The crocodile had no such problem. With a twitch of its tail it slid smoothly into the water; a second twitch sent it gliding powerfully towards the helpless girl. Its strong, slimy snout rose from the water as its jaws opened for the kill.

There was a bony crunch.

A heavy pistol thrown with great force had hit the crocodile right between the eyes. With a roar of pain and anger the crocodile turned away from the helpless Kate to discover who was daring to attack him.

But the crocodile turned too late; for the man who came to Kate's rescue was the man who was poised to rescue Daphne from the dummy crocodile. The Custard Kid found he had nothing left to throw. So with a rope in his hand he dived into the water and landed squarely on the animal's back.

The crocodile twisted his long nose around to snap at the stunt-man, but Custard was seated on its back with his arms around its throat.

The crocodile rolled; it dived and it lashed with its tail, but the Custard Kid still clung on like a barnacle on a ship's bottom. At last the animal made one tremendous effort to twist its head around to reach him. Custard grabbed his chance like lightning and dropped the noose of his rope over the rearing snout and pulled it tight.

Willing helpers at the side of the tank grasped the free end of the rope and pulled the crocodile out of harm's way while the exhausted Custard allowed himself to be dragged out of the water.

The Custard Kid took a deep breath and turned to look for Kate. She was standing at the edge of the water tank, sobbing and clinging

tightly to a man for comfort. It was Hunk Marvel, and Custard suddenly felt a little hurt. Hunk patted Kate's head and muttered calming words into her ear, then he looked up sharply. He stared hard at the Custard Kid and the look in his eyes was one of bitter hatred.

Startled, and a little puzzled, Custard turned away.

As he reached the door a hand touched him gently on the arm and a woman's voice said, 'Just a moment, Custard.' He swung round hopefully and found himself looking into the serious, kindly eyes of Miss Minnie Warmer.

'Oh, hullo, Miss Warmer,' said Custard politely, but secretly a little disappointed that it was not Kate.

'That was a very brave thing you did there, Custard,' she said, 'but there's one thing I don't understand.'

'What's that, Miss Minnie?' asked Custard, blowing at a huge drop of water that was collecting on the end of his nose.

'If you had a gun, why did you throw it at the crocodile? Why didn't you just shoot it?'

Custard blushed a little as he admitted, 'Well, I never carry bullets in the gun in case I have an accident. I have only blanks.'

Minnie Warmer thought for a moment, then said quietly, 'I think it might be a good idea if you were to load your gun with real bullets in future.'

'Of course Miss Minnie. If you say so.'

'It's just that I'm not too happy that the appearance of that crocodile was purely an accident,' she murmured thoughtfully.

'You mean . . .' gasped Custard.

Minnie interrupted him sharply. 'All I'm saying is that there have been a lot of "accidents" around here lately. Too many.'

'But why?'

'I think that somebody is trying to put Warmer Sisters out of business,' she replied simply. She then looked straight at him and said, 'Keep your eyes open, your gun loaded, and take special care of your friend Miss Kate.'

It was a sad and thoughtful Custard Kid who went back to his hotel to change.

But in the studio, there was a very happy director, Otto Premiere. His eyes shone contentedly as he turned to the cameraman, a little old man with the face of a leather-skinned gnome and the name of Sam Shine.

'Well, Sam,' snapped Otto Premiere, 'Did you get that rescue action?'

'Sure thing, Mr Premiere,' grinned Sam Shine. 'Much better than a wooden crocodile, and I got it all on film. *What* a scene!' he chuckled. 'What a *scene*!'

7

Suspicions

Later that afternoon Calamity Kate found Custard sitting thoughtfully outside the studio, in the sun. She rushed up to him and gave his bony body a hug that brought curious cracking sounds from his ribs. 'Oh, Custard,' she cried excitedly, 'you were just wonderful this morning. You saved my life and everyone's talking about how brave you were.'

'Oh, no,' mumbled Custard shyly. 'Anybody would have done the same.'

'Hunk Marvel didn't, and he was there,' replied Kate. At the mention of Hunk Marvel Custard's face became puzzled.

'I wonder why Hunk Marvel looked so annoyed that I'd rescued you?' he said slowly.

'Did he?'

'Yes. He was holding you in his arms,' said Custard (and he paused to let Kate take in his look of disapproval), 'then he looked at me as if he wished I were dead.'

'Maybe he was jealous because he likes to be the hero all the time. He likes people to notice him, but your rescue took all the glory away from him,' explained Kate.

'Then why didn't he rescue you himself?' snorted Custard.

'He wasn't there when the crocodile first attacked me. He just arrived while you were fighting it,' explained Kate. 'And anyway, he can't swim.'

'What was that you said?' asked Custard so sharply that she jumped a little.

'I said, Hunk can't swim.'

'No, before that. You said he wasn't there when the crocodile entered the water?'

'That's right,' answered Kate. 'Why?'

'Well,' Custard said slowly, 'I've been doing some investigating, and that crocodile didn't get there by accident.'

'But of course it was an accident,' said Kate nervously. 'What else could it have been?'

The Custard Kid repeated to Kate his talk with Miss Minnie Warmer about her suspicions that someone was out to ruin the studio. 'I then found out that the crocodile had been stolen from a local zoo. You were pushed into the water, then someone opened the trapdoor and let the crocodile into the studio tank.'

'How do you mean "someone"?' asked Kate.

'Someone who could have been at the back of the tank to open that trapdoor.'

'Surely you don't suspect Hunk Marvel?' gasped Kate.

'He could have opened that trapdoor, and he certainly wasn't very happy to see you rescued,' replied Custard grimly.

'But why?' asked Kate bewildered.

'I don't know but I mean to find out,' he replied.

'How can you be sure it's Hunk? He wasn't the only one who could have been there to open the trapdoor. Don't forget that Abel Sourgrape pushed me into the water then disappeared round the back of the set,' Kate pointed out.

The Custard Kid sighed. 'It's not going to be easy.'

Kate patted his hand gently. 'Never mind Custard, you'll find out who did it.' She blushed shyly and said, 'At least I know I'm safe while I have a real hero like you around to look after me.'

Custard jumped up suddenly with a cry of annoyance. 'That reminds me. I promised Miss Minnie that I'd look after you, and that I'd load my gun with real bullets just to be on the safe side.'

'Well?' asked the alarmed Kate.

'My gun is still at the bottom of the water tank. I'll go and fetch it now.'

'I'll wait here for you Custard,' called Kate as he strode into the studio, unarmed and unsuspecting.

8

Wall of Fire

Custard walked out of the glaring sunlight into the gloomy studio and blinked until his eyes became used to the dark. He slowly groped his way towards the water tank at the far end of the building and stared into the inky water.

'Hopeless,' he muttered. 'Can't see a thing. I'll have to switch some lights on.' Custard edged his way along the side of the water tank until he reached the lighting control room – a tiny cupboard so full of black buttons, silvery switches and wayward wires that he was terribly tangled in no time.

Suddenly a shaft of daylight shot through the studio as the door swung open. Custard caught a glimpse of a tall man – a black shape against the bright sunshine. The man seemed to be carrying

a can in each hand; he looked around quickly and closed the door.

Custard stayed silent in the dark of the control room.

He waited. And in the darkness at the far side of the studio the stranger seemed to be waiting too. Custard heard a clank as two cans were placed on the floor and, when he heard the harsh breathing, he realised that he had almost stopped breathing himself. Just at that moment the door opened again and a short, stocky figure slipped swiftly into the studio.

Through the heavy black air a rough voice grated, 'Have you got the gas?'

'Gas?' thought Custard. 'Why should anyone want gas? We use electricity here in the studio.'

'Two cans,' came the quiet drawling reply. 'Shall I switch the lights on?'

The rough voice grunted, 'We don't need light. By the time we've finished there'll be enough light in here.'

'And heat too,' came the drawling reply, followed by a snigger.

'Open the cans,' ordered the first voice. 'We'll take one each.'

The Custard Kid strained his ears and heard a gentle glugging of liquid from the cans, then a sharp, sickly smell stung his nostrils. He had smelt it once before when he had walked past Miss Gertrude Warmer's new motorcar. And a word floated into his mind. The word 'gas'.

'Cars run on gasoline – or "gas",' thought Custard, but try as he might he couldn't remember seeing a motor car in the studio.

The gurgling stopped and the 'bonk . . . bonk' of a couple of empty cans being thrown aside echoed through the studio. The two strangers dashed out.

Slowly the door creaked open.

And the Custard Kid watched open-mouthed as a pinpoint of light was sent spinning through the air. As the lighted match struck the floor there was a booming bang that hurt Custard's ears and a flash of flame that singed his eyebrows.

A wall of flame three metres high sprang up; a wall that stood between Custard and the door. A wall that crept steadily closer and turned Custard into jelly.

9

The Wall of Water

Calamity Kate opened her eyes with a start and had the uneasy feeling that something was very wrong. She had dropped off to sleep in the warm sun, but as soon as she awoke Kate knew that the Custard Kid had been gone too long. She rose slowly, stretched and took a deep breath – then she coughed. A wisp of smoke had tickled her throat and it thickened into a cloud of choking fumes.

'Oh, Custard,' she cried, when she saw that the smoke was pouring out of the huge wooden barn that served as a studio. Hitching up her skirts Kate rushed towards the building.

The thick smoke blotted out the sunshine and stung her eyes, so that Kate had to grope blindly for the door. She lifted the latch and pushed, but was horrified to find the door jammed by fallen timber. Kate lifted her large, unladylike boot and, with a kick that would have made a mule proud, she burst open the door.

Fresh air rushed through the open door to feed the furnace that faced her – it seemed to suck the very air from her lungs, leaving her just enough breath to gasp, 'Oh, Custard!' Tears left

white streaks on her smoke-blackened cheeks as she stood and panted helplessly at the door. The dazzling brightness of the fire hurt her eyes but still she couldn't tear her gaze away from the fierce glare.

Suddenly there was a huge roar and a deafening hiss as the flames disappeared and a cloud of steam swallowed Kate. A moment later a wall of water shook the side of the barn and gushed out through the only opening – the doorway. And in that doorway Kate had been standing.

The waist-deep river lifted Kate off her feet and dumped her in a puddle of water and sizzling wood at least ten metres from the door.

'Oooh!' gasped Kate as the roar of burning was replaced by the gentle hissing of water on charred wood. 'A miracle.'

From somewhere in the distance worried voices cried 'Fire!' and Kate heard footsteps hurrying to the scene. But her gaze was still fixed on the doorway.

In the blackness she saw a pair of eyes emerge. They blinked. A moment later a toothy smile appeared, and into the steamy sunlight stepped the sooty, but relieved, Custard Kid.

'You . . . you're still alive!' stammered Kate.

The Custard Kid looked himself up and down then gently patted his singed and smoking body. 'Looks like it,' he said, grinning cheerfully.

'But . . . but how?'

'The water tank,' he replied simply as he helped the trembling Kate to her feet. 'I took the axe from the railway rescue scene, knocked the side out of the water tank and let a few thousand gallons of water deal with the fire.'

By that time the first helpers had arrived on the scene, and Custard had to explain to them too just how he had escaped from the blaze. What Custard was careful not to mention was the fact that he knew the fire had been started deliberately.

He saved that knowledge for later that evening when he told the full story to Minnie Warmer and Otto Premiere who listened with very worried expressions on their faces.

'So,' murmured Minnie, 'someone *is* trying to ruin Warmer Sisters.'

'It looks as if they have succeeded,' growled Otto Premiere.

Minnie lifted her gentle blue eyes in surprise at this. 'Why do you say that, Mr Premiere?'

'It's obvious that we can't complete the film if we haven't got a studio to make the film in,' he replied bitterly.

'Oh, but surely the insurance company will pay to have another one built,' chipped in Kate desperately, as she saw her first chance to become a star slipping away from her.

'Yes, but not in time to save this film,' answered the director scornfully.

'Oh, I see,' muttered Kate humbly, even though she didn't.

'What Mr Premiere means,' explained Minnie Warmer gently, 'is that all the people working on *The Dangers of Daphne* are only here for a week or two. It would take at least six weeks to build a new studio, and by that time actors like Hunk Marvel and Abel Sourgrape, and Mr Premiere himself, will be off to make other films for other companies.'

'We can't afford to hang around for six weeks without pay,' grumbled Otto Premiere.

'And we can't afford to pay them for six weeks without a film being made,' said Minnie, completing the explanation.

'So,' snapped Otto Premiere to Minnie Warmer. 'The wreckers have succeeded.'

'No,' replied Minnie quietly.

'But ...' blustered the director impatiently, until Minnie's firm quiet voice silenced him.

'We will film the remaining scenes on location,' she explained simply. Otto Premiere sank back in his chair and stroked his chin thoughtfully.

'You mean we film the railway rescue scene on a real railway track with a real locomotive?' asked Custard.

Minnie nodded.

'Won't that be a little dangerous?' queried a quivering Kate.

'Hmm,' answered Minnie. 'That's our other problem. We must find the wreckers and put a stop to their little game.' She turned a keen eye on Custard. 'Do you think *you* could deal with them young man?'

Custard thought of the savage crocodile attack on the innocent Kate and his face looked grim as he replied, 'I most certainly can, Miss Minnie.'

She turned next to Kate and said, 'It will be dangerous. Are you prepared to risk it?'

Kate thought of the glamour of completing the film against all the odds and becoming a star; with a slight tremble in her voice she replied, 'I certainly am, Miss Minnie.'

Lastly Minnie turned to Otto Premiere. 'Can you make a film without a studio?'

Otto Premiere thrust out his chin proudly and declared, 'I can do anything. But the film will *not* be as good as one made in a studio!'

The faces of the other three fell a little in disappointment, then a gleam came into the eye of the director and a smile turned up the edges of his mouth.

'It will be *better*!' he cried.

10

Black-bearded Bert

Calamity Kate shivered in the chilly dawn air as she lay across the railway track and allowed her hands and feet to be tied to the cold steel rails. She turned her head stiffly to look along the track to where the locomotive with its two coaches steamed and snorted in readiness.

'What happens if the train doesn't stop?' she asked nervously.

'Don't worry, Miss Kate,' replied Hunk Marvel soothingly. 'Bert will tie special knots in the ropes so that you only need to give a light tug and they'll come loose.' He nodded at the stage-hand who was tying Kate's wrist at the time.

'Sure thing Mr Marvel,' replied Bert in a harsh whisper. 'There you are, try that Miss Kate.' She gave a sharp tug at the rope and it came away easily.

'Oh, that's all right then,' she said cheerfully.

'I'll just tie it up again,' grated Bert. As Bert bent over Kate, his thick black beard brushed against her nose and made her want to sneeze. She sniffed deeply to clear her nose of the tickling feeling and was overpowered by a strong scented smell.

'Oh my!' she thought to herself. 'That Bert has certainly used strongly-scented shaving soap this morning.'

'O.K. Bert, go and check the brakes on the train now,' ordered Hunk Marvel, much to the annoyance of Otto Premiere who liked to give all the directions himself.

Mr Premiere glared at Hunk and said sharply, 'Now listen everyone; these are *my* instructions.' He turned to explain to the camera crew and to Minnie Warmer who had just arrived.

'Camera One will shoot the train rushing down the track. Camera Two will, at the same time, film Miss Kate trying to free herself. Then we'll stop the train and film the scene showing Hunk Marvel rescuing Miss Kate by slicing through the ropes with an axe. Is that clear?' he asked, glaring around him.

‘Yes Sir,’ everyone mumbled.

‘Get into your right positions then,’ he snapped. The cameramen hurried to obey. One ran 400 metres up the track to film the approaching train, while Sam Shine moved in close to film Kate’s struggles. The Custard Kid moved uneasily away to stand well back from the scene beside Minnie Warmer and Hunk Marvel.

‘Cameras roll!’ called Otto Premiere, and he waved a large red handkerchief for the driver of the train to start. Nothing happened.

A small figure climbed down from the engine and ran down the track to where Otto Premiere waited looking very cross. It was the young fireman from the locomotive who came up panting and explained, ‘Sorry Mr Premiere, sir, but there's been a slight delay.'

'Delay?' said the scowling director. 'What sort of delay?'

'The brake coupling was leaking and one of your stage-hands, a guy with a big black beard, spotted it,' replied the fireman. He mopped his sooty brow with an even sootier handkerchief.

'Delays cost money,' snapped Otto Premiere. 'How long will it take to repair?'

'Oh, your stage-hand is working on it now!' answered the fireman cheerfully and he turned to go. He stopped when he reached Hunk Marvel. 'Say, aren't you Hank Wonderful?' he asked, wide-eyed.

Hank gave one of his famous handsome grins and drawled, 'Well, almost. The name's Hunk Marvel.' The Custard Kid blinked thoughtfully as he heard the smooth, slow voice of the film star – he had heard that voice somewhere before.

'Could I have your autograph Mr Marvellous?' chirped the happy fireman.

'Well . . .' began Hunk.

'Get back on that train *now*,' roared Otto Premiere, and the shaken little fireman scuttled back to his waiting locomotive.

'Right, let's try again,' muttered the director. Aloud he called in his powerful voice, 'Scene 31, take 2. Cameras roll!' Again he waved his handkerchief, and this time was rewarded with a cloud of steam and a powerful 'Chooof... chooof... chooof...' as the train set off and began to gather speed.

At that moment something clicked in the Custard Kid's mind – he remembered where he had heard that drawling voice of Hunk Marvel's before; and it was not a happy memory. He looked at Hunk and saw a cruel smile flickering across his lips. Then, with a shiver, Custard looked up to see the train rushing down the track towards his friend, Calamity Kate. He loosened his gun in its holster.

At almost the same moment something clicked in Kate's mind – 'If that stage-hand had a beard, then why did he smell so strongly of shaving soap? A man with a beard doesn't shave!' she reasoned. 'If he's wearing a false beard then he must be a fake . . . and I let him tie me to this track!' Kate stopped *pretending* to struggle and began to *really* struggle.

'O.K. cut!' shouted Otto Premiere. He waved a handkerchief to signal to the engine driver to stop a hundred metres short of where the kicking Kate lay.

The driver spun the brake wheel sharply and was surrounded by a cloud of steam. 'The brake pipe's been cut,' cried the young fireman, and the train hurtled down the slope towards the actress.

Kate kicked loose the ropes around her feet and tore her left wrist free from the rail. The train was just fifty metres away from Kate as she scrambled clear of the track and tugged at the trick knot in the rope around her right wrist. But it wasn't a trick knot.

Her hand was tied firmly across the rail.

'Cut!' gasped Otto Premiere and felt sick as he realised what he had said.

The train was just twenty metres from parting Kate and her hand. She leaned back with all her strength to pull her hand free from the rope. The rope burned her wrist but refused to let go of its prize. With the front wheels of the locomotive just ten metres from the screaming girl, the Custard Kid calmly drew his gun, pointed it carefully towards Kate . . . and fired.

11

The Plotters Plan

The bullet cut through the rope like a knife through water. Kate tumbled backwards and before she touched the dusty ground the runaway engine roared past.

Everyone sighed with relief as Calamity Kate picked herself up and dusted herself down. Her face was pale and her knees were shaking as she walked over to Custard, put her arms around him and rested her head weakly against his chest.

The first person to recover from the shock was Sam Shine, the old cameraman, and he was almost dancing with excitement. '*What* a scene, Mr Premiere. What a *scene*!'

The Director's eyes lit up as he turned to the little man. 'You got all that on film, Sam?'

'I certainly did, Mr Premiere!'

'Terrific!' gloated the director. 'This will be the most exciting film ever made,' he crowed.

'It won't!' The quiet but determined voice of Kate silenced him. A red spot of colour darkened both cheeks and an angry fire lit her eyes. 'I'm not going on,' she stated flatly.

'But, Miss Kate . . .' argued the director impatiently.

'No. I've nearly been killed twice and Custard has almost died too. It isn't worth it.' Suddenly her eyes filled with tears. She turned and ran off in the direction of the town.

The Custard Kid turned to go after her but a light touch on his arm stopped him. 'Bring Miss Kate along to my office this evening, and we'll discuss this calmly,' said Minnie Warmer. Custard nodded and hurried after Kate.

. . . . . .

Four worried people sat around the lamp-lit table in Minnie Warmer's office that evening.

After they had talked for two hours Minnie summed up what they knew. 'Two people are trying to ruin Warmer Sisters. One is this mysterious "Bert" and the other is. . . .'

'Hunk Marvel,' said Custard.

'I still can't believe it,' said Kate.

'I can,' said Otto Premiere.

'There was the way he looked so annoyed when I rescued you from the crocodile,' explained Custard to Kate. 'It was *his* voice I heard when the studio was set on fire, and it was Hunk who gave the order for Bert to tie you to the track,' he went on.

'Hmm,' said Minnie thoughtfully, 'a glance, a voice in the dark and an order don't prove anything.'

'And that's one of the things we need ... proof,' said Otto Premiere.

'One of the things?' queried Custard.

'Yes. We also need to know who this "Bert" really is, and we need to know *why* they are doing this,' he replied.

'And now we'll never know,' said Minnie Warmer with a twinkle in her eyes.

'But we have to!' cried Kate in alarm. 'We have to!'

'We can't if you don't want to go on with the film,' answered Minnie wickedly.

'Of course I'm going on with the film,' Kate exclaimed, jumping to her feet and thumping the table vigorously. 'I'm not going to be done out of my stardom by a couple of crooked, crackpot cut-throats. I'll show them that when they mess with Calamity Kate they've bitten off more than their cup of tea.' She sat down with a satisfied bump.

Custard, Minnie and the director exchanged secret smiles and Otto Premiere said seriously, 'Are we to understand Miss Kate, that you have changed your mind about quitting the film?'

'You bet!'

'It will be dangerous for you,' warned Minnie.

'It will be more dangerous for that "Bert" character when I get my hands on him!' she answered fiercely.

'In that case,' said Minnie looking around calmly at the others, 'we need a plan.'

And so it was that four determined plotters put their heads together around a smoky oil lamp and made a plan.

12

The Sawmill Scene

Kate tiptoed nervously into the deserted saw-mill. 'Is anyone here?' she cried out pitifully. The only answer was a faint echo of her feeble voice as it bounced off a huge steel circular saw.

Kate took a deep breath and peered nervously round a pile of logs. There was no one there. 'Oh dear!' she exclaimed. 'He promised to meet me here, but I do believe that he has let me down.' She was just about to look behind a stack of planks when she heard a floorboard creak. Kate spun round quickly, but saw no one. Then, from behind the stack of planks, a black-gloved hand reached out and wrapped itself around her mouth.

Kate kicked and struggled but Abel Sourgrape was too strong for her. As he dragged her over to the circular saw he leered wickedly at her and chuckled, 'This will put an end to all your schemes, my beauty.' Suddenly his expression changed from pleasure to pain. 'Yaaaa-Oooo! She bit me!' he cried as Kate sank her teeth into the gloved hand.

He angrily moved the injured hand and wrapped a cruelly tight arm around Kate's throat; he threw her across the workbench in front of the saw and tied her hands and feet with black cord.

'O.K. Cut!' called Otto Premiere.

Sam Shine stopped the camera and grinned happily. 'Oh boy, Mr Premiere, that looked real!'

Kate struggled to sit up and glared angrily. 'It was real,' she said. 'He hurt me.'

Abel Sourgrape fumed as he carefully pulled the glove off his hand. 'It certainly was real,' he said. 'She bit me!' He stalked to the door, turned round and said, bitterly, 'Amateurs!' before striding out.

It took Otto Premiere a few minutes to calm Kate, then he made an announcement. 'I want everyone to leave the sawmill for a few minutes while I check Miss Kate's ropes. This is the last danger scene of the film and we don't want any more accidents ... do we?' he asked looking hard at Hunk Marvel. The film star gave a sneering smile in reply, but walked out with the others.

Five minutes later they returned to see Kate lying very still across the circular saw bench, her red shoes just showing under the hem of her blue-check dress. Her head was dangling out of sight at the far side of the bench.

The Custard Kid was sent up to a gallery where the controls of the saw were situated. The director gave his final orders. 'Custard will start the saw. When it is one foot away from Miss Kate he will stop the saw. Hunk Marvel will then rush in with his axe, cut the cords and drag Miss Kate clear.'

Minnie Warmer slipped into the sawmill and stood by the door watching quietly as the saw roared into life. Sam Shine cranked his camera while Otto Premiere breathed heavily at his shoulder and Hunk Marvel stood testing the edge of the axe with his thumb and smiled to himself. Abel Sourgrape had not returned to the sawmill.

All eyes were on the saw as it moved slowly closer to Kate's unmoving body. Its huge teeth glinted wickedly in the powerful electric flood-lights and Minnie felt an uncomfortable shiver though she knew that everything was under control. With the saw just thirty centimetres away from ripping into the lifeless form on the bench Otto Premiere called, 'Stop the saw, Custard!'

The saw whirred on.

Everyone turned and looked up at the control room. The Custard Kid lay slumped across the controls and a stocky, bearded figure was just disappearing through a door which led from the gallery to an outside staircase. The saw was just ten centimetres from the body on the bench when the director called urgently to Hunk Marvel, 'Cut the ropes with the axe!'

With a faint smile Hunk Marvel strolled slowly over to the bench – much too slowly. When he reached it the saw had begun to tear the blue-check dress to shreds and bite deeply into the body.

Otto Premiere ran swiftly up the steps to the control room, switched off the whining saw and lifted Custard's head. Slowly the stuntman blinked, then carefully touched a very tender swelling on the back of his head. 'A man,' he gasped painfully. 'A man with a beard . . . .'

'Just sit and rest until you are strong enough to come down,' said Otto Premiere quietly. 'Everything went to plan except....'

'Except I let "Bert" get away,' Custard finished.

'True,' agreed Otto Premiere thoughtfully. 'We are up against a very clever criminal ... still, no harm done this time,' he went on cheerfully. Custard felt the growing lump on his head and wasn't so sure about that!

'You can come out now, Miss Kate!' Otto Premiere called down.

From behind a log stack Calamity Kate emerged and walked over to the mangled shape on the bench. She tugged at the straw stuffing which filled her shredded dress, and felt very shaken. Without the plan which her friends had worked out last night it would have been Kate inside that dress.

Two people in the room did not know about the plan to put the dummy in place of Kate. One was Hunk Marvel, who smiled bitterly and said, '*So* pleased to see you are not hurt, Miss Kate,' before walking out of the sawmill.

The other was little Sam Shine who stood bewildered beside his camera and said weakly, '*What* a scene, Mr Premiere ... but ... but I think I'm going to faint....'

And he did.

13

Custard's Curtained Corner

The final scene of *The Dangers of Daphne* was the big romantic scene in which the hero (played by Hunk Marvel) asked Daphne (played by Kate) to marry him.

Otto Premiere hired the ballroom of the Golden Ritz Hotel for the day as the Warmer Sisters' studio was a charred ruin after the fire. At one end of the ballroom the stage-hands built a set to represent Daphne's humble cottage; at the other end, the lights and cameras were placed.

Behind the cameras, waiting and watching, sat the Custard Kid. He sat in a dark corner, his back to thick velvet curtains, feeling just a little jealous of Hunk Marvel as he watched the handsome star whispering loving words to Kate.

'Oh, Daphne,' he declared with a voice like honey. 'Three times have I saved your life. Now I ask a simple reward . . . .' He stared deeply into her eyes and Kate felt her heart flutter as it had the first time he had stared into her eyes, but there was a difference. This time her heart fluttered with fear. Fear of the man who had plotted three times to kill her.

'Will you marry me?' crooned Hunk Marvel. Kate sat still, her mouth frozen stupidly open. For a long moment the only sound in the ballroom was the whirring of Sam Shine's camera as everyone held their breath, waiting for Kate to give Daphne's loving reply to the proposal. But she didn't move or utter a sound.

'Will you marry me?' repeated Hunk with the hint of a threat in his voice. He reached forward and took Kate's hand.

Kate moved. Kate made a sound. She jumped up and screamed, 'Aaagh . . . Oooh . . . let go, you horrible man!'

'Cut!' roared Otto Premiere so loudly that it shocked Kate into silence. The director clenched his teeth and tried to keep his temper.

'Miss Kate . . . you are supposed to be *Daphne*. You are *supposed* to accept Hunk's offer and kiss him.'

Kate stood trembling in front of him and looked very small and helpless. 'I'm sorry, Mr Premiere, I'm sorry. I . . . I lost my head. I'll do the scene again.'

Otto Premiere's heart softened at the pitiful sight and, to everyone's surprise, he turned to dismiss the studio workers. 'I think Miss Kate is still very upset as the result of the recent "accidents". We'll have the rest of today off and try again tomorrow.'

Minnie Warmer took charge of Kate and hurried her off to one of the hotel rooms to rest. Hunk went home and the studio hands began to take the set apart so that the ballroom could be used for dancing that evening.

But, in one corner, the Custard Kid was still sitting, thinking. Ever so slowly the curtain behind him moved. A harsh voice whispered, 'Hunk!'

'I . . . .' began Custard.

'No, don't say anything, just listen,' grated the voice. The Custard Kid realised someone had mistaken him for Hunk Marvel . . . and from the rough voice and the odd scented smell Custard guessed that the voice belonged to the mysterious 'Bert'. And 'Bert' was saying some very interesting things.

The voice grated on. 'The insurance money for the burnt-out studio will be delivered tomorrow. That will be fifty thousand dollars each. But it isn't enough. We get a million dollars when Miss Kate dies. This time, I'll make sure that the pointy-nosed, snooping Custard Kid is out of the way. You deal with Miss Kate. Understand?'

The Custard Kid nodded his head slowly. He no longer needed to turn round to look at 'Bert' – he knew who 'Bert' was, but he didn't know how to prove it.

Suddenly the curtain swished open again and the voice hissed 'Just one more thing. Get hold of the film of the runaway train. Destroy it!'

Custard nodded, and, as 'Bert' disappeared for the last time, he kept on nodding, satisfied.

'And now I know how to prove it!'

14

A Criminal Confesses

Otto Premiere called a meeting for everyone in the Warmer Sisters' office at eight o'clock that evening, but told no one the reason. Hunk Marvel agreed to attend but seemed very nervous; Abel Sourgrape complained bitterly about the waste of his precious time and Gertrude Warmer objected that she 'had better things to do'. But Otto Premiere was firm and at eight o'clock the unwilling trio turned up and took their places around the room alongside the curious Minnie Warmer, Calamity Kate and Sam Shine.

Otto Premiere wasted no time in getting down to business. 'Ladies and gentlemen,' he said,

looking around sternly, 'you are all aware that there have been some very unpleasant accidents around this studio during the past week. It is my sad duty to inform you that they were not "accidents" but deliberate attempts on Miss Kate's life.'

'Nonsense,' snapped Abel Sourgrape. 'Just the sort of bungling you would expect with amateurs.'

The colour rose in the director's cheeks as he replied sharply, '*I* am not an amateur, Mr Sourgrape, and the Custard Kid has *proof* that the attacks were deliberate.'

Hunk Marvel drew in his breath sharply and he looked far from handsome as his eyes narrowed and his lips curled in a vicious sneer. 'Proof! What sort of proof?'

'Your friend "Bert" told me about your plans to kill Kate and to share the insurance money. You see "Bert" mistook me for you,' explained Custard.

'The fool!' spat Hunk Marvel, then a cunning smile came over his face. 'Still, Bert is a long way away from here by now. Without Bert's evidence you've got nothing on me.' He stood up and backed towards the door. 'So, I think I'll just be getting along to join him now.' He opened the door, but didn't take his eyes off the shocked faces in the room. 'Oh, yes, I was in the plot to kill Miss Kate, but I didn't lift a finger to harm her myself. Bert did all the dirty work; stealing the crocodile, tying her to the track and knocking out Custard in the sawmill.'

'But you helped,' said Otto Premiere quietly.

'Yes,' hissed Hunk Marvel.

'And you helped to burn the studio,' went on the director.

'I did, but you still have no proof.'

'The Custard Kid was in the studio when you set it alight.'

'It's his word against mine,' said Hunk, his voice rising as he became more desperate.

'But you've just admitted it!' said the director.

'To you, yes, but you won't get me admitting it to the law.'

'True, true,' said Otto Premiere very pleasantly, 'which is why it's just as well the sheriff heard you admit it.'

'Ha!' Hunk snorted, 'What sheriff?'

'The one who's standing right behind you and who has been listening to every word you said since you opened the door.'

Hunk started for a moment then recovered his nerve. 'Nice try Mr Premiere, but I used that trick myself in the film *High Midnight*. As soon as I turn around to look for this imaginary sheriff you'll draw a gun on me.'

Otto Premiere shrugged his shoulders to admit defeat and smiled sadly. 'Alas Hunk, you're too smart for us. You are quite right. The sheriff is *not* standing behind you . . . are you sheriff?'

'No Sir,' came the deep voice of the sheriff . . . from behind Hunk Marvel.

The sneering smile slid off Hunk's face and he sagged like a sausage that suddenly loses all its stuffing. He sank down on the nearest chair, put his head in his hands and made no effort to resist as the sheriff slipped on the handcuffs.

'Oh, Hunk, why did you do it?' asked Minnie Warmer, sad and bewildered.

He stared back at her blankly.

'Will he go to prison for long?' asked Gertrude Warmer in a choked voice very different from her usual booming.

'That's for the judge to say, Ma'am,' answered the sheriff.

'Oh, it isn't fair!' exclaimed Kate, almost in tears. 'Why should Hunk take all the blame when that nasty "Bert" gets clean away?'

'And what makes you think "Bert" will get away?' asked Otto Premiere.

'But . . . but Hunk said. . . .'

'Hunk was bluffing. He may be a greedy fool, but you have to admire his loyalty. He could have given "Bert" away when he knew the game was up, but he didn't.'

'Then you know who "Bert" really is?' asked Kate with a gasp.

The director nodded and a strange smile crossed his face as he said, 'I know *who* Bert is; and I know *where* Bert is.'

Kate's voice was almost a whisper as she asked, 'Where?'

Otto Premiere paused a long time, before replying, 'Here in this room, Miss Kate. Here in this very room.'

15

Bert Un-bearded

In the crowded office of Gertrude and Minnie Warmer you could have heard a feather drop. Otto Premiere looked around the room and everyone shuffled uneasily wondering if they were sitting next to a dangerous ruffian who, disguised as 'Bert', had already tried to kill three times. The Director turned to his little cameraman and said simply, 'Sam, the film.'

Sam Shine turned down the oil lamp and switched on a small projector, which threw an image of a steam locomotive onto the white office wall. Otto Premiere exlained: 'We always take more film than we need for any scene. We allow the cameras to run for awhile *before* the scene begins and to run on *after* the scene is finished. That way we don't miss anything important. We can always cut the film and throw some away if we have too much, but if we missed something, then we would have to waste a lot of time shooting the entire scene again.'

The picture on the wall showed a small figure climb down from the cab of the locomotive and run down the track. 'That's the fireman, isn't it?' asked Minnie Warmer.

'That's right. He's on his way to tell me that the brakes need to be fixed. He also told me that one of my stage-hands had offered to fix them. In fact that stage-hand disconnected them!'

'Bert?' asked Kate.

'Bert,' said Otto Premiere. Everyone strained their eyes to examine the flickering picture and saw a stocky, bearded figure climb between the engine and the tender, then unfasten a steaming pipe. The figure gave a thumbs-up sign to the driver and stepped out of sight behind the train.

'But we *still* don't know who this Bert *is*,' complained Kate.

'One moment, Miss Kate. Remember I said that we allow the cameras to run on at the end of the scene too,' said the director patiently.

Kate turned back to the moving picture and saw the young fireman climb back to his cab and the train set off on its uncontrolled rush down the slope. Kate gave a shudder as she remembered that she had been tethered in the path of that huge iron monster. The engine and then its two coaches passed out of sight of the camera. As it passed it revealed once more the figure of Bert.

As the audience watched, breathless, Bert put a hand to the false beard and, carefully unhooking it from behind each ear, pulled it free.

'Stop the camera,' ordered Otto Premiere.

There, projected onto the wall was the face of the mysterious Bert; it was a face they all knew. It was the face of Gertrude Warmer.

'Not "Bert", but "Gert",' murmured the Custard Kid.

16

The Sisters' Slipping Success

Gertrude Warmer was led away without saying a word; the sheriff took with him two prisoners and left behind a room full of confused and unhappy people.

'But *why*?' asked Kate.

'Money,' answered Otto Premiere simply. 'The studio was going bankrupt very quickly, and Gertrude decided that the best way to make a lot of money fast was to insure an actress for a huge amount of money, then make sure she had a very nasty accident.'

'And they picked me,' said Kate.

'I didn't know that we were so short of money,' said Minnie weakly. 'Gertrude never told me anything about the business side of Warmer Sisters.' She sighed. 'Gertrude and I were never as close as we should have been. We're only step-sisters you know; she's the daughter of my father's second wife.'

'I should have guessed business wasn't so good when I smelt her perfume,' said Kate. Everyone looked at her curiously and she had to explain. 'No lady should wear as much cheap perfume as she did.'

'But why was the company so short of money?' asked the puzzled Custard.

Otto Premiere sighed. 'Mainly because she insisted on paying huge sums of money to Hunk Marvel for his acting. At first he was quite successful; he was very good looking and the public flocked to see him. But really he was just a handsome *dummy*! He couldn't act very well, and you can't fool the public for long. After a while people realised that he *wasn't* acting; he was just being himself – and that became very boring. So the public stopped going to see his films. Warmer Sisters were losing money on Hunk's films faster than they could have burned it.'

Everyone sat thoughtfully for a while, then Kate asked, 'Then why didn't you sack Hunk Marvel, Miss Minnie?'

'Gertrude wouldn't let me,' she replied heavily.

'But why?' persisted Kate.

Minnie Warmer looked a little guiltily over the top of her spectacles, and said quietly, 'Because Hunk was her son.'

'Her son!' exclaimed Otto Premiere. Then he nodded wisely, 'I see. I see now.'

'Gertrude was married when she was young, before my father met her mother. As she grew older and plainer her handsome actor husband left her. All she had left to live for was her son. She would do anything for her son to succeed. Even ruin the studio.'

'And it looks as if she *has* succeeded in doing that,' said Abel Sourgrape bitterly. Minnie nodded sadly in agreement.

'No!' cried Otto Premiere with fire in his eyes. 'I'm not going to sit back and see this studio ruined. We have a film to complete. It's called *The Dangers of Daphne* and with Miss Kate in the leading role and with a fine artist like Abel Sourgrape as the villain it is sure to be a great success.'

'But we don't have a leading man to play the hero,' objected Minnie Warmer.

'But we do!' replied Otto Premiere. He jumped to his feet and walked quickly over to Sam Shine who was re-winding film in the projector. 'Sam! How often does Hunk Marvel appear in the scenes from *The Dangers of Daphne* that we've filmed so far?'

Sam scratched his chin thoughtfully and replied, 'Well to be honest, not a lot. It's the Custard Kid who has done most of the work so far.'

'Exactly!' exclaimed the director happily. 'It's Custard who saves Daphne from the crocodile and it's Custard who saves her from the train. Custard can easily fill in the other scenes – he's watched Hunk do them and he certainly can't be any worse.'

'But I'm not an actor, Mr Premiere,' said the confused Custard.

'Neither was Hunk Marvel,' replied the director wickedly. 'I'm going to make you a star, my boy!'

17

The Big Romantic Scene

Daphne's humble cottage was rebuilt in the ballroom of the Golden Ritz Hotel and while the stage-hands put the final touches to the scenery the actors stood thoughtfully in the corner talking earnestly with Minnie Warmer.

'So you see,' Minnie said, 'the insurance company will drop the charges against Hunk and Gertrude if I agree not to claim the money for the fire.'

'But then you'll have to pay for a new studio yourself,' said Custard.

Minnie's eyes twinkled warmly. 'If this film is as successful as Mr Premiere says it's going to be, then I'll be able to build a hundred new studios.'

'So, you're dropping the charges?' asked Kate.

Minnie nodded. 'The only charge against them now is that of trying to kill you, Kate.'

Kate looked troubled. 'Oh, but they didn't do a very good job of it. They couldn't, while I had a real live hero like Custard around to protect me.' (The Custard Kid blushed so deeply at this remark that a red glow shone through his pale stage make-up.) 'And anyway, I always felt so sorry for Gertrude . . . well, what I mean to say is, can't *I* drop the charges against them too. They won't try to harm me again now.'

'You're a very generous girl, Kate,' replied Minnie. 'I'll visit the sheriff and see what I can do.'

Kate was about to offer to go with Minnie when the stern voice of Otto Premiere called out, 'Right, let's have the actors on the set.'

Minnie Warmer gave Kate's hand a quick squeeze and said, 'Good luck, my dear. I'm sure you'll have no trouble with the big romantic scene this time.'

Now it was Kate's turn to blush and mutter, 'Why, Miss Minnie, I don't know what you mean!'

'Come along, Miss Kate,' chided the director. 'Time costs money. Remember that, time costs money.'

Kate grinned happily at Otto Premiere's scowling face, gave him a huge wink (much to Sam Shine's amusement), then ran over to the set of Daphne's cottage where Custard was waiting for her. She looked affectionately at her old friend and said warmly, 'You know, Custard, I really think you're better looking than Hunk Marvel anyway!'

'Quiet on the set!' roared Otto Premiere.

'Sorry Mr Premiere,' said Kate meekly.

'Final scene; take two,' called Mr Premiere.

The hero looked deep into 'Daphne's' eyes.

'Cameras roll.'

The hero edged closer to Daphne on the sofa.

'Action!'

The hero breathed deeply then began his proposal to Daphne. 'Oh Kate,' he declared in a voice so like a real lover that even Otto Premiere didn't notice the mistake. 'Oh, Kate,' he sighed.

'Three times have I saved your life. Now I ask a simple reward....' Kate (or was it Daphne) looked up and met his eyes encouragingly. 'Will you marry me?'

'Of course, stupid,' replied Daphne (or was it Kate?).

'Now you have to kiss her,' ordered the director. 'That's right ... camera fade out ... now cut! That's the end of the film. That was a much better scene than the one you performed with Hunk.... Er, Miss Kate... I said "Cut"... you can stop now, Custard.... Oh, never mind!'

'Amateurs,' grumbled Abel Sourgrape with a chuckle.

'*What* a scene!' declared Sam Shine. 'What a *scene*!'

The End